For Jonathan Squire
M.A.

For Caroline and Sam
M.F.

First published in Great Britain in 1990
by Simon & Schuster Young Books

Simon & Schuster Young Books
Simon & Schuster International Group
Wolsey House
Wolsey Road
Hemel Hempstead
Herts. HP2 4SS

Set in 16pt Bembo Roman educational by
Goodfellow & Egan Phototypesetting Limited, Cambridge
Printed and bound in Belgium by Proost International Book Production

British Library Cataloguing in Publication Data
Andrew, Margaret
  Nanook the Polar Bear
  I. Title   II. Foreman, Mark
  823 (J)
  ISBN 0-7500-0211-5
  ISBN 0-7500-0221-2 Pbk

Also written by Margaret Andrew and published by Simon & Schuster Young Books:

Mac the Macaroni — the penguin who liked to dance
Illustrated by Tracey Lewis
Mac the macaroni is not like other penguins. Mac likes
to dance, and dance he does as he sets off on this
dazzling adventure set in Antarctica.
Hardback ISBN 0 356 13733 3   **Paperback** ISBN 0 356 13734 1

NANOOK
THE POLAR BEAR

by Margaret Andrew
illustrated by Mark Foreman

SIMON & SCHUSTER

LONDON • SYDNEY • NEW YORK • TOKYO • SINGAPORE • TORONTO

Once, during a long, dark winter in the far north of Canada, three polar bear cubs were born in a snow den. Their mother called them,

Big Nanook,

Middle Nanook

and Little Nanook.

The cubs enjoyed snuggling by their mother and suckling her warm milk.

After some weeks Mother Nanook said,
"It's time to go outside into the big world.
Don't worry while I'm gone."
She scraped and cleared snow from a tunnel
and off she went out of sight.

Soon she called to the cubs one by one.
Big Nanook and Middle Nanook lost no time
in scrambling up the snow tunnel.
Then it was Little Nanook's turn.
He pulled himself forward up the slippery slope
but kept sliding back.
"Come on!" called Mother Nanook.

By the time Little Nanook had hauled himself out
and managed to open his eyes against the light,
he saw the other two cubs playing.
Mother Nanook licked him and gave him some milk.
"You'll soon get used to it," she said.
"The first place we must go to is the . . .

SEA."

Down the hill they walked, one behind the other.
Soon the cubs were playing by the sea,
batting at bits of ice and sliding down slopes
on their stomachs.
The sun shone and warmed them.
Little Nanook watched the seal pups play and
was very happy.

Some days later, Mother Nanook began to teach them
how to crouch low and creep along the snow,

and how to hide behind an ice hummock
beside a hole.

One day a young seal came up for air and
Mother Nanook cuffed it with her paw,
hauling it from the water.

She watched the cubs.
Big Nanook and Middle Nanook sniffed
the dead seal and began to eat it.
But Little Nanook sat to one side
and looked away.
"How will you grow big and strong
if you won't eat?"
Mother Nanook asked him.
"I like the seals," Little Nanook replied.
"I don't want to eat them."
So Mother Nanook slid into a pool and
brought up a great, fat . . .

FISH!

Big Nanook and Middle Nanook fell upon
the fish and ate it in a flash.
Little Nanook did not get any.
"You must be quicker," said Mother Nanook.

That day Little Nanook went hungry.

The weeks went by as the cubs played outside during the day and slept in the den at night. Big Nanook and Middle Nanook grew more and more as they ate the seals their mother caught, while Little Nanook stayed the same small size.

"You must hunt for yourselves
now you are older,"
Mother Nanook told them.
"You first, Big Nanook."

Big Nanook crouched low
and caught a young seal.

"Good," said Mother Nanook.
"Now you, Middle Nanook."

Middle Nanook lay by a pool
and scooped up a fish.
"Very good," Mother Nanook told her.

"Now it's your turn, Little Nanook," said his mother.
"What are you going to hunt?"

"I'm not hunting by the sea,"
said Little Nanook.
"I can smell something exciting and
I'm going to find it."

Then away he ran, across the
hard ground of the tundra,
at such speed the others had to
run hard to keep up with him.

Suddenly they heard 'sik-sik'
and a small, furry animal
appeared in front of them.
It was a . . .

GROUND SQUIRREL.

"Run, Little Nanook, run!" shouted Mother Nanook.
Little Nanook did run. He ran right past the
ground squirrel. He was after something
but that was not it.

The ground squirrel ran down a hole.
"Oh, dear!" Mother Nanook exclaimed.
"You must do better than that."
"You'll never catch anything if you go past it!"
shouted Middle Nanook.
"What I'm hunting isn't found here,"
said Little Nanook.

He put his nose up and
sniffed and sniffed,
and sniffed!

Just then, a large bird flew from the scrub.
It was a . . .

PTARMIGAN!

"Go!" shouted Big Nanook.

"I am going," replied Little Nanook
but he did not stop to catch the bird
and the ptarmigan escaped over their heads.

On ran Little Nanook until
a small animal jumped into the air.
"That's it! That's what he's hunting,"
cried Mother Nanook. "It's a . . .

LEMMING!"

"No, not a lemming," Little Nanook
called back over his shoulder.
"I don't want to hunt those funny
little things. I'm going to find what
smells so good."

Big Nanook and Middle Nanook
were getting cross for they were becoming
hungry. Mother Nanook growled at them.
"Can't you smell something?" asked Little Nanook
as he reached the top of a hill and paused.
"We can't smell *anything*," they replied,
"except . . .

GROUND SQUIRRELS,

PTARMIGANS

and LEMMINGS!"

"There *is* something else," cried Little Nanook,
"and we are almost there!"

He waved his upturned nose as he sniffed and
took to his heels again. He ran over a slope
so fast that they lost sight of him.

And when the other bears reached the
top of the hill and looked down –
there he was, in the middle of lots of . . .

BERRY BUSHES!

His chest was stained pink as
the juice ran down his chin.
"You see," he called, "I've found what I like best."

"What a clever bear!" exclaimed Mother Nanook,
as they ran to join him.
"Berries are a bear's favourite food."

Big Nanook and Middle Nanook were
too busy eating to speak.
They had never tasted anything so delicious.

So Little Nanook did not have to hunt seals,
after all. He ate,
FISH
   GRASS,
      ROOTS and . . .
         lot and lots of BERRIES!

Author's note

Usually two cubs are born to the female polar bear during her time in the den. However, in some parts of the Arctic, triplets have been seen. When born the cubs are the size of guinea pigs, from 15–30 centimetres in length and about a kilogramme in weight. For three weeks the mother bear keeps them off the icy ground, lying on her fur. The cubs have very sharp claws so they can cling to her.

Cubs stay with their mothers in dens for about ten to twelve weeks and at the end of this time, they are so fit and strong after being suckled by her rich milk, they are ready to go outside. At night they return to the den (*iglooviuk*).

When the mother emerges from the den, she will look to see if there are any male bears in the area. Male bears can attack young cubs and the mother bear may take her family inland to avoid them.

Although the sea is the polar bears' usual hunting place and seal their main food, they go elsewhere at times to eat grasses, roots and small animals. They are reported as having a great liking for berries of all kinds; cranberries, crowberries and blueberries.

Tundra is the name given to the bare, wind-swept country of the Arctic, which may have grasses, lichens and small wild plants growing on it.

Nanook (Nanuk) is the Inuit name for polar bear.